The

Traveling Ball of

String

story by *Mary Calhoun*
pictures by *Janet McCaffery*

William Morrow & Company 1969

Published simultaneously in Canada by
George J. McLeod Limited, Toronto.

Printed in the United States of America.

Library of Congress Catalog Card Number 69-15042

You know the old saying,
"Use it up, wear it out,
Make it do, do without."
Well, the Widow Tuckett was like that.
Widow Tuckett was the savingest woman.
She saved old newspapers and jar rings,
bottles and scraps of cloth,
picture cards
and the combings from her hair.
She didn't throw anything away.
Try to get her to toss something out,
she'd say,
"No, I just might want that someday."

String, though, that was her prize.
Widow Tuckett was the best string saver
these hills have ever seen.
She had a ball of string
that was the seven-days' wonder
of the county.

Talk about a pile of string!
Big as a rain barrel, only fatter around.
She kept it out in her washroom,
sitting in a patch of sun,
and folks would come by
just to look at that ball of string.

Got so the widow just loved to see
a bit of string come her way.
At the store she'd say,
"Just tie that parcel up
with a little piece of string."
Then she'd take it home,
tie the string
onto the last strand in the ball,
and wind it in.
'Course, she'd use the string, too.
She'd go out to her ball, all smiling,
because she knew

right where she could lay a finger
on a bit of string.
Seems like that widow-woman
purely made a pet of that ball of string.
They say she was as cozy with her string
as an old lady with her cat.
Sometimes, when she was washing,
she'd talk to it like it was a cat.
"Well, String,
gonna be nice weather today, I see."
When she cut off a length, she'd say,
"Thank you, String."

And when she tied on another piece,
she'd smooth down the strands
and pat them
and tell the whole thing
how it was a nice old ball of string.
People'd tell her,
"You oughta show that ball
at the county fair."
Then she'd chuckle and say,
"Yes, I should."

Never did, though.
No proper division for it.
Well sir,
at the time I'm telling you about,
the ball of string had grown so big
it took up half the washroom,
like to crowd the widow out.
She couldn't bear the thought
of putting her string out in the barn,
where it couldn't keep her company.
So she took out a wall of the washroom
and build on a lean-to shed.
Even cut windows in the lean-to,
so the string could sit in the sun.
Got all done,
she pushed the string into place and said,
"There now, honey.
There's you a new shed to sit in,
all nice and handy to me."

Wasn't really a *new* shed, though.
She built it out of some old boards
she'd kept lying around,
knew they'd come in handy someday.
So maybe the boards were rotten.
And, being a widow-woman,
maybe she wasn't so clever at nailing.
Another thing, she hadn't leveled
the ground under the shed,
so the ball was sitting on a slope,
leaning against the wall.
Anyway, whatever the reason,
one day that ball of string
went on a rampage.

Widow Tuckett was out in the tomato patch
when it happened.
Way she tells it,
she heard the boards of the lean-to
creaking and giving.
Then the walls burst open,
and the string came rolling out.
And down the steep hill
that ball went a-tumbling away.

Widow Tuckett picked up her skirts
and took off after it, yelling,
"Come back here, you ball of string!"
The ball just rolled on
down through the woods,
gathering speed,
like a house a-coming down the hill,
crunching over bushes,
bouncing off of trees.
Old Man Wicker was in the woods
gathering mushrooms,
and the ball of string
plumb knocked him cat-west.

Next it landed out on the road,
good straight downhill road.
Then that string began to build up
a real head of steam,
roaring down the pike,
knocking gravel every which way.
Along behind came the widow,
apron strings flying.
Up ahead were some folks in a wagon,
going to town.

"Stop my string! Stop my string!"
yelled the widow.
"Look out for the string!
Look out for the string!"
yelled the folks,
jumping out of the wagon.
Bump, bounce, the ball just trundled
right over the wagon.
Down through the creekbed
and right smart up the next hill
chugged the ball of string.
But near to the top
she lost her steam
and started to roll back.
"Here comes the string!
Here comes the string!"
squawked the folks,
who'd started to climb
back in their wagon.

"Catch my string! Catch my string!"
yelled the widow.
Some smarty little boys
were up on the hill.
"Help the string! Help the string!"
says they.
And they gave the ball
a little heave over the top.
"There goes the string!
There goes the string!"
the boys shouted, dancing about.
That was all the string needed.
It tore off downhill to the village,
straight for
the church ladies' annual open-air bazaar
and strawberry festival.

Yessir, all that hoorah was spread out
there on tables at the bottom of the hill.
Didies and doilies
and fancy-made pincushions
and all the geegaws
that women fix up to sell,
plus buckets of ice cream
and tubs of strawberries
in their sweet, sticky syrup.
And people all over the place,
having themselves a holiday.

Right straight for it all
came the ball of string,
plastered with mud and gravel and leaves,
rolling and tumbling,
roaring and rumbling.
And tearing along after it,
the widow and the little boys
and the wagon folks, yelling,
"Look out for the string!
Look out for the string!"

Smack through the bazaar
came the ball of string.
Splashed through the strawberries,
didn't miss the ice cream,
rolled down the tables,
picking up didies and doilies
and fancy-made geegaws
that stuck to the strawberry syrup.
Folks scattered like marbles,
and horses reared in the air,
screaming
at the sight of the awful thing.

One horse was particular scared.
It took off with its buggy
still hitched on behind
and a poor little child sitting in it.
"Runaway horse!" cried the crowd.
"Save the child!"

That old ball of string,
it just bounded right on,
straight into the path of the horse.
Fetched itself up against him
with a whump
and knocked the runaway
clean out of that horse.
Knocked the horse down in its stays,
so he just lay there
a-whickering and a-whimpering.

The mother of the child ran out
and grabbed it, crying,
"Saved my child! It saved my child!"
"Always knew
that string would come in handy someday!"
said Widow Tuckett.
She'd finally caught up,
and she panted and puffed
while she patted the string, all smiles.
Saved a child! Think of that!

Her ball of string was a hero!
She always knew
it'd come in handy someday.
That's what she told everybody
who'd listen.
Then she rolled her ball home,
it dropping doilies along the way.
Still, it had enough bazaar stuff
plastered into it with syrup
that it was a regular treasure trove.

The Widow Tuckett
was picking out plunder for days.
At last she got her string all tidied up,
braced the shed wall,
put back her ball,
and there it sat
till the Widow Tuckett died.
Never did go a-traveling again.
They say there was talk
of putting the ball
on the widow's grave for a monument,
but nothing came of it.
For all I know, it's still sitting there
in the shed in the sun,
that wonderful ball of string.